This Boxer Books paperback belongs to

. . . .

For Monica Jean Allen - 1929-2007
J.A.

First published in hardback in Great Britain in 2008 by Boxer Books Limited.
First published in paperback in Great Britain in 2010 by Boxer Books Limited.
www.boxerbooks.com

A CIP catalogue record for this book is available from the British Library upon request.

ISBN 978-1-907152-52-8

1 3 5 7 9 10 8 6 4 2

Printed in Slovenia

All of our papers are sourced from managed forests and renewable resources.

I'm not Santa!

Jonathan Allen

Boxer Books

It was Christmas Eve, and Baby Owl
had been out in the snowy woods,
playing on his sledge.
The woods are so quiet in winter,
he thought as he trudged home.

"Santa!" called Baby Hare. "It's you!"

“I’m not Santa!” said Baby Owl.
“Don’t be so silly.”

“But you are Santa,”
insisted Baby Hare.
“You’re wearing a red hat with fur on it. Santa wears a hat like that.”

“But I’m not Santa!” said Baby Owl.
“I’m an owl.”

“You’re big and fat like Santa,”
cried Baby Hare.
“You are Santa!”

“I am not Santa!” said Baby Owl.
“And I am not big and fat like Santa.
I’m very fluffy like a baby owl.”

"You are Santa!" Baby Hare wailed.
"You've got a sleigh.
Santa's got a sleigh."

"I am not Santa!" cried Baby Owl.
"And it's not a sleigh, it's a sledge.
Sleighs are much bigger.
And I'm an owl."

"But you are Santa," said Baby Hare.
"You keep saying you're not,
but you are."
And Baby Hare started to cry.
"Waaaaah."

"Please don't cry, Baby Hare,"
said Baby Owl.

"WAAAAAAH,"

howled Baby Hare.

"Oh, all right," cried Baby Owl.

"I am Santa! OK?

I'm Santa! Ho, ho, ho!

Just stop crying, please."

Baby Hare stopped crying.
He looked at Baby Owl.
"You're not Santa," said Baby Hare.

"Santa's got a big beard, and he wears
big black boots with fur round the top."

Baby Hare started to cry again. "You said you're Santa, but you're not," he wailed. "Waaaaaaah."

Now Baby Owl was upset.
"I only said I was Santa to stop you getting upset and crying," he wailed.

"And now you're crying again.
It's not fair. Waaaaaaah."
And Baby Owl burst into tears.

"What's all this crying and carrying on?"
Said a big, jolly voice.
"And at Christmas time too."
"Santa!" cried Baby Hare.
"Santa!" cried Baby Owl.

"Now, come and give me a hug and
let's have no more of this crying,"
laughed Santa.

"Mum," cried Baby Owl. "Baby Hare thought I was Santa but I'm not and he started crying and then I said I was Santa to stop him crying and he started crying again because he said I wasn't Santa, and then Santa came along and cheered us both up. Wasn't that brilliant?"

“Yes, dear,” said Mum.

“And now it’s time for bed, Baby Owl.”

“Here’s your Christmas stocking, Baby Owl,” said Mum, when she’d read him a story and tucked him in. “We’ll hang it at the end of the bed. Goodnight, and sleep tight.”

“Goodnight, Mum,” said Baby Owl.

“Goodnight, Owly, and Merry Christmas.”

Other Boxer Books paperbacks

First Snow • **Bernette Ford & Sebastien Braun**

It is cold for early winter. Snow begins to fall – first slowly – big flakes softly falling, melting fast. Bunny and his brothers and sisters leave their cosy burrow to explore this shimmering, glistening new world. The discovery of winter's first snow is beautifully captured in this enchanting and poetic story.

ISBN 978-1-905417-14-8

Jingle-Jingle • **Nicola Smee**

It's snowing and the barnyard is filled with excitement at the prospect of a sleigh ride with Mr Horse. Cat and Dog and Pig and Duck are all ready to go – but Mr Horse wants to ride in the sleigh too! Get ready for a seasonal ride that every toddler will want to join again and again!

ISBN: 978-1-907152-57-3

Mine, All Mine! • **Claire Hawcock & Chiara Pasqualotto**

When Little Squirrel finds a beautiful, shimmering snowflake, he wants to keep it all to himself. He builds himself a tree house and hides away with his wonderful find. But as time passes and he begins to feel lonely, Little Squirrel realises his treasure would be even more wonderful if he shared it.

ISBN: 978-1-907152-55-9